WORLD IN VIEW

CENTRAL AMERICA

Marion Morrison

THOMPSON STATION

RAINTREE
STECK-VAUGHN
LIBRARY
The Steck-Vaughn Company
Austin, Texas

© **Copyright 1993, text, Steck-Vaughn Company**

Library of Congress Cataloging-in-Publication Data

Morrison, Marion.
    Central America / Marion Morrison.
       p.   cm.—(World in view)
    Includes index.
    Summary: Surveys the history, geography, culture, economics, and daily life of the seven countries that comprise Central America.
    ISBN 0-8114-2458-8
    1. Central America—Juvenile literature. [1. Central America.] I. Title. II. Series.
F1428.5.M67   1992   92-14537
972.8—dc20   CIP AC

Cover: *Painted church in San Andres Xecol, Guatemala*
Title page: *Quiché-Maya of Chichicastenango, Guatemala, at the Sunday market.*

Design by Julian Holland Publishing Ltd.

Consultant: Bruce Taylor, University of Dayton

Typeset by Multifacit Graphics, Keyport, NJ
Printed and bound in the United States
by Lake Book, Melrose Park, IL
1 2 3 4 5 6 7 8 9 0 LB 96 95 94 93 92

Photographic Credits
All the photographs are from South American Pictures and are by Tony Morrison except the following: 5, 9, 21, 30, 74, 88 Jevan Berrange; 40, 82 Marion Morrison; 81, 84 Garry Willis.

Contents

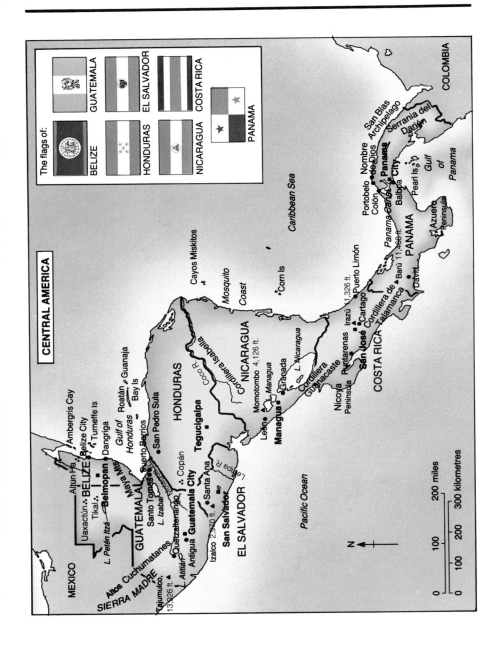

1   A Land Bridge

Central America consists of seven of the smallest countries in Latin America: Panama, Costa Rica, Nicaragua, Honduras, El Salvador, Guatemala, and Belize, formerly the self-governing colony of British Honduras. Together they are smaller than the state of Texas and occupy the narrow strip of land, or isthmus, that connects the continents of North and South America. The eastern seaboard of Central America faces the Caribbean Sea, which is part of the Atlantic Ocean, and on the western side lies the Pacific Ocean. El Salvador is the only country without a Caribbean coastline.

Costa Rica has a varied tropical coastline. At Golfito, on the Pacific coast, the shore is sheltered by the Osa Peninsula.

Many millions of years ago the landmasses of North and South America were separated by

5

water. They were gradually connected, some three to four million years ago, as a result of movement of the huge plates that make up the earth's surface. Violent friction between two of these plates, the Cocos and the Caribbean, created volcanoes and mountains, and eventually the stretch of land that is now Central America. As a land bridge, it is a unique meeting place for all kinds of animal and plant life from the two great continents and is the route through which the first inhabitants migrated from north to south. Geographically, the mountainous countries of Central America are similar, but the low, hot, and wet Caribbean coast contrasts markedly with the drier, steeper Pacific coast.

Central America is also important from a global standpoint, because its narrow width in the region of the Isthmus of Panama provides the

The Countries of Central America

	Capital	Area	1988 Population	Currency	Language
Belize	Belmopan	9,186 sq mi (22,965 sq km)	179,000	Belize dollar = 100 cents	English (Spanish also spoken)
Costa Rica	San José	20,400 sq mi (51,000 sq km)	2.85 million	Colón = 100 centímos	Spanish
El Salvador	San Salvador	8,416 sq mi (21,041 sq km)	5.1 million	Colón = 100 centavos	Spanish
Guatemala	Guatemala City	43,556 sq mi (108,889 sq km)	8.7 million	Quetzal = 100 centavos	Spanish (some Indian languages also spoken)
Honduras	Tegucigalpa	44,835 sq mi (112,088 sq km)	4.1 million	Lempira = 100 centavos	Spanish
Nicaragua	Managua	51,550 sq mi (128,875 sq km)	3.62 million	New Córdoba = 100 centavos	Spanish
Panama	Panama City	30,833 sq mi (77,082 sq km)	2.32 million	Balboa = 100 centésimos	Spanish

shortest crossing for shipping between the Atlantic Ocean on the east side and the Pacific Ocean to the west. The alternative route around Cape Horn is about 1,800 miles. A canal large enough to take oceangoing ships between the Caribbean Sea and the Pacific Ocean was started in Panama in 1881, but it was not finally opened until 1914. Due to the *S* shape of the isthmus and the difficulty of constructing the Panama Canal through a gap in the mountains, entry to the waterway on the Atlantic side lies west of the exit on the Pacific side. So the passage from the Atlantic to the Pacific is, surprisingly, in a west-east direction, not east-west as would be expected.

The mountains
The mountains of Central America are broken up into many different branches, sometimes called *cordilleras* from the Spanish word "chord" or "chain." In Costa Rica, for example, there is the Cordillera Central, the Cordillera Guanacaste to the northwest, and the Cordillera de Talamanca to the southeast; in Guatemala there are two parallel mountain ranges, the Sierra Madre and the Altos Cuchumatanes; and in Belize the southern part of the country is dominated by the Maya Mountains. The proportion of mountainous land differs within each country, ranging from about 75 percent in Honduras and almost 90 percent in El Salvador to just 15 percent in Panama. Most of the highest peaks in Central America are volcanoes, some active, and many mountains reach altitudes of 8,000 to 10,000 feet (about 2,400 to 3,000 meters).

The mountain slopes are covered in rich, varied forests. At the lowest level, to an altitude of about 3,000 feet (910 meters) and mostly facing the Caribbean Sea, is dense tropical rain forest, with tall trees, thick undergrowth, and tangled masses of vines and lianas. Facing the Pacific coast at about the same level, the forests have both deciduous and evergreen trees, with expanses of open woodland and grassy plains, or savannahs. Higher up the slopes on both sides of the mountains, there are forests of large oaks and pines. Above an altitude of about 5,000 feet (1,515 meters) there are "cloud forests," where the trees are permanently soaked in mist and many colorful flowers, such as orchids, and other plants, such as bromeliads grow. In recent years large areas of the forest have been destroyed for commercial purposes.

The volcanoes

Central America has many volcanoes, and more than 30 are active. The majority are on the western (Pacific) side of the isthmus. In Guatemala, an impressive chain of 33 volcanoes in the southern Sierra Madre includes the highest mountain in Central America, the volcano Tajumulco at 13,926 feet (4,220 meters). Also within this group is Tacaná at 13,507 feet (4,093 meters) and the three active volcanoes of Pacaya, Fuego, and Santa María. To the south of Guatemala, El Salvador has over 200 volcanoes, 14 of which are over 2,970 feet (900 meters). The most famous of these is Izalco, also known as the "Lighthouse of the Pacific," which last erupted in October 1966.

The land of Central America is dominated by many active volcanoes. Arenal in Costa Rica is 5,356 feet (1,623 meters) high.

There are more than 40 volcanoes in Nicaragua, 6 of which are currently in some stage of activity, including the famous Momotombo. In 1835 the country experienced massive explosions from the volcano Consigüina that were heard as far away as the Caribbean island of Jamaica and in northern South America. Debris from the eruption covered villages and farms over a wide area. Other volcanic eruptions in 1902 killed nearly 40,000 people.

Costa Rica's principal volcanoes stand not far from the capital city, San José, and it is possible to visit Irazú (11,326 feet, 3,432 meters high) and the huge smoking crater of Poás by paved road. Between 1963 and 1965 Irazú was so active that it threatened to ruin the nation's coffee crop. In

9

Tremors and earthquakes occur frequently in some parts of Central America. In 1972 Managua, the capital of Nicaragua, was almost totally destroyed.

Panama the dormant volcano Barú (11,468 feet, 3,475 meters) is the country's highest peak.

Central America suffers frequently from earthquakes. The capital city of Guatemala has been damaged or destroyed 9 times, and that of El Salvador 14 times. In 1972 Nicaragua's capital, Managua, was almost completely flattened. In 1976 the region experienced its most devastating earthquake when more than 20,000 people in Guatemala lost their lives.

Highland plains and valleys
In the mountainous regions many towns and villages have developed in valleys and on plateaus. Some were originally established to be close to mines, but the majority owe their

existence to the richness of the soil and the potential for agricultural production. Deposits of volcanic lava and ash, and the fallout of eruptions have made the land in some of these regions particularly fertile. Crops of many kinds can be grown. Depending on altitude, these include coffee, sugarcane, wheat, and other crops. The land is also good for raising cattle. In Guatemala the valleys average between 5,000 feet (1,524 meters) and 8,500 feet (2,590 meters) in altitude. In El Salvador they are generally lower, with the capital city of San Salvador, in a fertile semitropical valley beneath the towering San Salvador volcano, some 2,244 feet (680 meters) above sea level.

Among the capital cities founded on plateaus are Guatemala City, which is located on a central plain between the Sierra Madre Mountains and the Altos Cuchumatanes, and San José in Costa Rica, which is on the Meseta Central, an ash-covered plain at the foot of the Cordillera Central Mountains. The Meseta Central covers an area of 2,080 square miles (5,200 square kilometers) and lies at an altitude of about 3,016 feet (914 meters).

The coasts

The hot and humid lowlands on the Caribbean side of Central America are seldom more than 50 miles (80 kilometers) wide. They are crossed by many rivers flowing from the mountains into the Caribbean Sea, creating swamps, lagoons, and small deltas where mangrove swamps are abundant.

In places the low-lying coastal zone has beautiful white-sand beaches, often fringed with coconut palms. Only along the easternmost part of the Honduras coast and northern Nicaragua, in the region known as the Mosquito Coast, are the lowlands wider. The Mosquito Coast takes its name from the Miskito Indians who lived there, but owing to the dense forests and exceptionally heavy rainfall, the whole area was largely neglected until early in the twentieth century. At that time, huge banana plantations were developed over large areas.

Some coral reefs and several islands lie off the Caribbean coast. The world's second-longest coral reef, after Australia's Great Barrier Reef, belongs to Belize. It is surrounded by dozens of small islands, called *cays*, with beautiful sandy beaches and clear water excellent for swimming and diving. Honduras owns the Bay Islands in the Gulf of Honduras, of which the hilly Roatán is the largest. Guanaja, the most eastern of the group, was named the Island of Pines by Christopher Columbus, and many tall pine trees still grow there.

Off the Nicaraguan coast are two small, pretty islands, fringed with white coral and slender coconut trees, known as the Corn Islands. At the southern end of the isthmus, 365 small and large islands make up the San Blas Archipelago, which belongs to Panama and is home to the colorful Cuna Indians.

Along the Pacific coast there are numerous swamps, creeks, bays, gulfs, and peninsulas such as Nicoya in Costa Rica and Azuero in Panama. The Pacific coastal zone is at most half the width of the Caribbean coastal zone, and although it is forested in many parts, extensive regions are cultivated. The capital of Panama, Panama City, is on the Pacific side of the isthmus, and in the Gulf of Panama is the largest of the Panamanian islands, Coiba, together with Taboga and the historic Pearl Islands.

Petén and Darién

At either end of the isthmus are two large territories that are almost uninhabited. In the north, extending over about one-third of Guatemala, is a limestone tableland called the Petén, covered largely by dense jungles of hardwood forest and some flat grassland, with woods and streams. During the rainy season the land is dotted with lakes and ponds, which drain into underground caverns. Fewer than 50,000

These Mayan temples at Tikal in the tropical forests of Guatemala are among the tallest ancient buildings in the Americas.

13

people live in the Petén. The main town, Flores, is built on an island in the middle of Lake Petén Itza and has a population of 5,000. It can be reached, with difficulty, by road, and there is a small airport. Yet once it was the home of the Mayas, one of the most remarkable early peoples to inhabit the isthmus, and ruins of their great cities and temples today lie hidden in the tangled rain forest.

In the south a largely unexplored region called the Darién covers almost half the country of Panama and joins the isthmus to northern South America. The region contains incredibly dense vegetation and is threaded with rivers and streams. It is one of the wettest places in the world and was once thought to harbor head-hunting natives. The region is completely undeveloped, without roads or towns, and the only inhabitants are small groups of Cuna and Chocó Indians and some black descendants of African slaves. Only a handful of well-equipped expeditions have forged their way through the Darién, and anyone wishing to get from Panama to South America travels by air or sea.

Lakes and rivers

The western region of Nicaragua is a land of freshwater lakes. Lake Nicaragua, covering some 3,300 square miles (8,288 square kilometers), is the largest in Central America. The lake contains a number of islands large enough to house people and villages, and on one, Isla Ometepe, there is a perfectly shaped volcanic cone rising to 5,313 feet (1,610 meters). Lake Nicaragua drains into the San Juan River, which passes through deep jungles to the east and flows for 120 miles (193 kilometers) before entering the Caribbean in the northern corner of Costa Rica. This lake and river network has often been considered as a possible alternative to the Panama Canal. Although Lake Nicaragua is a freshwater lake, sharks and other saltwater fish can be found there because they swim up and down the San Juan River.

Connected to Lake Nicaragua by the Tipitapa River is Lake Managua, with the capital city Managua on its western shore. Only a fraction of the size of Lake Nicaragua, but famous for their beauty, are the lakes of Atitlán and Amatitlán in southern Guatemala. They are ringed by volcanoes, and the color of the water constantly changes to a variety of deep blues and greens as the sun changes the colors of the mountain peaks and sky above them. Atitlán in particular is spectacular. Guatemala's largest lake, Izabal, is in the Caribbean lowlands.

The longest rivers in the isthmus are those that rise in the mountains and flow into the Caribbean Sea. These include, in Nicaragua, the Coco River (or Segovia) with a total length of 424 miles (684 kilometers), part of which forms the border with Honduras, and the 200-mile (322-kilometer)-long Matagalpa River.

In Guatemala the Motagua River crosses the country from west to east and reaches the sea after 250 miles (402 kilometers), the last 100 miles (160 kilometers) of which are navigable. The Reventazón River, which drains from the Meseta Central in Costa Rica, also flows into the Caribbean. Many shorter rivers descend into the Pacific, including the two most important in

El Salvador, the Lempa and the Grande de San Miguel, and no less than 350 in Panama. Panama has a total of some 500 rivers, but despite a considerable increase in the volume of water during the rainy season, very few are navigable.

The main rivers of Belize are the Hondo River, which forms the border with Mexico in the north, and the Belize River, which crosses the center of the country and on which the old capital of Belize City stands. Rising in the north of Guatemala and forming part of its border with Mexico is the Usumacinta River, which flows almost 700 miles (1,127 kilometers) before emptying into the Gulf of Mexico.

Rain and winds

Central America lies in the tropics, but only the lowland regions experience a typically hot and humid tropical climate all year round, with temperatures averaging between 85°F and 90°F (29°C and 32°C) during the day. In the mountains, altitude affects the temperature, although nowhere does the temperature normally drop below 50°F (10°C), and that only at nighttime at altitudes above 6,000 feet (1,829 meters). The contrast between hot daytime and cooler nighttime temperatures becomes more marked as altitude increases.

To distinguish the different mountain zones and temperatures, local people refer to the level from the lowlands to about 3,000 feet (910 meters) as the *tierra caliente,* or hot lands; the level from 3,000 to 6,000 feet (910 to 1,800 meters) as the *tierra templada,* or temperate lands; and above 6,000 feet (1,829 meters) as the *tierra fria,* or cold lands.

Cattle are raised throughout Central America. These cattle on the dry western side of Costa Rica are being driven to market in Punta Arenas.

Because temperatures remain much the same throughout the year, the seasons are defined by the amount of rainfall. Although rain at any time is not uncommon, the drier season occurs between December and April and is more pronounced on the Pacific coast. Many parts of the Caribbean coast are subject to considerably heavier rainfall than the Pacific, a fact clearly demonstrated in towns on either side of the Panama Canal. Whereas Colón on the Caribbean side has an annual rainfall of 129 inches (3,220 millimeters), Balboa on the Pacific side, only 40 miles (64 kilometers) to the south, has 70 inches (1,750 millimeters).

Several countries in Central America have been hit by hurricanes. In 1961 Hurricane Hattie partly

17

destroyed Belize City; in 1974 Hurricane Fifi caused widespread damage and serious flooding in Honduras; and in 1988 Hurricane Joan devastated parts of the Caribbean coast of Nicaragua, leaving 300,000 people homeless.

Wildlife

The unique position of Central America as the link between the ancient lands of North and South America has given it a rich variety of wildlife. When the two huge landmasses were isolated from each other, different animals evolved in each region. Among those in the north were carnivores, including early jaguars and pumas, and in the south some unusual animals such as opposums, armadillos, and anteaters. Until the land connection was made, all these land mammals were confined to their original homes. Once the land bridge was formed, these animals migrated north and south. The South American monkeys are one exception. They

The Resplendent Quetzal

One of the most elegant birds in the entire world, and certainly the most striking in the Americas, is the resplendent quetzal, a pigeon-sized bird. The male is adorned with beautiful feathers of green and red, and has three-foot-long tail plumes. The quetzal inhabits the mountain forests of Central America, and for a thousand years or more it was the sacred bird of the early Central American civilizations. Now it is the national bird of Guatemala and its image adorns coins and bank notes.

A jaguar rests in a clearing deep in the rain forest. It is the largest cat in the Americas, and an adult can weigh up to almost 300 pounds (135 kilograms).

probably evolved from a northern ancestor that managed to cross the ocean-filled gap, possibly using islands like giant stepping-stones to reach the southern continent. Monkeys similar to those in South America, such as spider monkeys, howler monkeys, capuchins, and squirrel monkeys, are commonly seen in today's Central American forests.

A short, late afternoon walk in the protected forest around Tikal in the Petén reveals just how richly varied and abundant the animal life can be. Coatis, the long-tailed relatives of the raccoon, scavenge for insects and fallen fruit. Small light-brown foxes break cover to cross a glade, while armadillos, agoutis (small rodents), and deer keep to the undergrowth. Traces of jaguar and a

19

smaller relative, the ocelot, are not uncommon. Birds, more than 250 species of them, are everywhere. Toucans, parrots, and macaws are in the forest canopy; tinamous, partridge-like and well camouflaged, run between the tree roots. Only in parts of northern South America is the bird life as abundant as it is in Central America, where the enormous range of habitats has provided an exceptional variety of food and shelter.

Of the amphibians and reptiles, perhaps the most colorful are the brilliant red or orange thumbnail-size frogs of the higher rain forests. These are poison arrow frogs, so called because some Indian tribes at one time made a deadly poison from glands in the frog's skin. Also notorious is the fer-de-lance snake. This pit viper has such powerful venom that it has been given the name "three step." It is said that after being bitten, the victim takes three steps before falling. Fortunately, such instances are rare.

2   Early History to Independence

The first peoples to inhabit the American continent probably arrived some 20,000 years ago, having migrated from Asia across the Bering Strait near the end of the Ice Age. They may have overlapped with the great herds of grazing animals, such as mammoths, mastodons, and giant bison, but there was also plenty of smaller wildlife and wild plant foods to help them survive.

By about 2000 B.C. the early American inhabitants had the knowledge to cultivate

Solid stone spheres have been discovered in Costa Rica. No one is sure of their origin, although it has been suggested that they belonged to the Dignis culture sometime between 200 B.C. and A.D. 1550. Their purpose and significance are unknown.

various crops, including corn, beans, squashes, and pumpkins, and there is evidence that they produced stone tools for food processing and some pottery, basketry, and small figures made of clay. Instead of living as wanderers, they began to settle in communities. Archaeologists, who study the past, have found proof of village occupation in various places, including Las Charcas in Guatemala, dating from that time. In the centuries that followed, more advanced civilizations began to emerge in the region known to archaeologists as Mesoamerica. For cultural and geographical reasons, Mesoamerica includes Mexico and the countries of Guatemala, Belize, and the northern parts of El Salvador and

The Footprints of Acahualinca
Near the old center of Managua in Nicaragua, at Acahualinca, workers digging for building stone chanced upon some footprints left on dried mud that was once the edge of an ancient lake. The footprints had been protected by a thick layer of volcanic rock and ash spewed from a nearby volcano. Closer examination revealed that the footprints were those of men, women, and some animals, including a deer and possibly a jaguar, and that they were thousands of years old. Archaeologists have puzzled over the mystery because the people appear to have been running to the lake, with some footprints much deeper than others, as if some of the people were carrying heavy bundles. One explanation may be that they were fleeing from the erupting volcano, but until further excavation takes place, no one can be sure.

Honduras. The most remarkable civilization was that of the Maya.

The Maya

The Maya were outstanding in many different ways. They were excellent builders, sculptors, and potters. They developed an advanced knowledge of mathematics and astronomy, which they used to calculate accurate calendar years. They also developed a system of writing, and they achieved considerable success in the planting and harvesting of many cultivated plants.

Early Mayan peoples settled on the Pacific coast close to the Mexican-Guatemalan border, and in the highland region around Kaminaljuyú on the western outskirts of Guatemala City. The civilization reached its height between about A.D. 400 and A.D. 900, when it occupied the Petén lowlands and extended into all of modern Guatemala's neighboring countries. Among the many huge cities built by the Mayas are Tikal and Uaxactún in the Petén, Altun Ha in Belize, Tazumal and San Andrés in El Salvador, and Copán in Honduras. Tikal covering an area of more than 6 square miles (16 square kilometers) was perhaps the most impressive, with huge pyramids that even today rise above the canopy of the surrounding forest. One of the highest pyramids is the Temple of the Giant Jaguar, rising 145 feet (44 meters) above the central Great Plaza.

The Mayas moved many tons of earth and rock to construct their cities, yet they had no knowledge of the wheel, and they had no beasts of burden. Their tools of stone and obsidian, a black, volcanic glass, were simple, but many walls and "stelae," or upright stone columns, are decorated with fine carvings full of intricate detail, showing scenes of daily life or images of gods. Some of the carvings are hieroglyphs, a form of picture writing, which the Mayas also made into books called codices, made of a form of bark paper. Archaeologists do not yet understand all the hieroglyphs, but they have deciphered some information about Mayan ruling families.

Much more is known about the Mayan method of counting, which included the idea of zero, an idea not used by either the ancient Greeks or Romans. The Mayas devised one calendar year of 365 days. They also developed a solar calendar, which they consulted to organize their agricultural year and, combined with astronomy, to predict important events.

Warring states

The Mayan civilization was made up of city-states, often at war with each other, and with no single city in control. Each was ruled by hereditary nobles and priests, while the people worked on the land or as artisans in thatched huts around the cities. No one is quite sure why, but sometime between the eighth and tenth centuries A.D. the Maya civilization in the lowlands declined. The constant fighting must have been a factor, although it is also possible that the land could no longer support a large population.

After the eleventh century, the Mayas survived in the highlands of Guatemala, particularly in the city-states of the warring Cakchiquel and Quiché-

The Mayas played a ball game they called pok-a-tok. *Ball courts, like this one at Tikal in Guatemala, were built in many places and would have been crowded with spectators.*

A Mayan Game

Within many of the cities the Mayas built ball courts, and there is an excellent example in Copán. The courts were large and rectangular in shape, with high walls on all sides and seats for spectators. The object of the game was to get a ball, made of heavy rubber, through a small stone ring set high in the wall, maybe 23 feet (7 meters) above the ground. The players wore protective clothing, but as they could touch the ball only with their thighs, hips, and elbows, the game was clearly very strenuous.

Maya Indians, and they had contact with the Toltecs and Aztecs of Mexico, who sent merchants into Mayan territory for cacao (to make chocolate, which was a favorite Aztec drink), quetzal feathers, jade, and shellfish. Mayan influence is thought to have extended to southern Nicaragua, but other groups of Indians were scattered throughout Central America. The Pipils were originally traders from Mexico, and there were Pipil-speaking Indians the length of the

Pacific coast. Other Indians, mainly wandering or nomadic hunters and fishermen, included the Lenca in Honduras, the Suma on the northern border of Nicaragua, the Miskito on the Mosquito Coast of the Caribbean, the Guaymí in Costa Rica, and the Cuna and Chocó in Panama. These were the people living in Central America when the Spaniards arrived.

The Spanish Conquest

Among the first explorers to sight the coast of Central America around the beginning of the sixteenth century were Alonso de Ojeda, Rodrigo de Bastidas, and Christopher Columbus. It was only on his fourth voyage in 1502 that Columbus landed in Honduras and in Panama, which he named Veragua. In 1510 survivors of two expeditions to the Gulf of Darién, who had met fierce resistance from the natives, founded the first real European settlement in the New World, Santa María la Antigua del Darién. Among their number was Vasco Núñez de Balboa. Balboa is remembered as the first man to cross the isthmus, an extremely difficult expedition through jungles full of hostile natives and dangerous animals. He accomplished this with 190 men in 18 days. When he reached the Pacific Ocean in 1513, he claimed it in the name of the king of Spain.

Balboa did not have long to celebrate his triumph, as he was beheaded by the ruthless Pedro Arias Dávila, better known as Pedrarias, who had been appointed governor of the region by the Spanish monarchy. Pedrarias himself crossed the isthmus in 1519 and founded the city of Panama, and it was in the same year that

Hernán Cortés began his conquest of Mexico. The future of Central America lay in the hands of these two ambitious men, each of whom was anxious to be the first to conquer the territory. Pedrarias sent expeditions north from Panama, and Cortés sent his men south from Mexico City. Both sides encountered desperate resistance from the natives, who greatly outnumbered the Europeans, but the Spaniards were hardy, ruthless, and determined. Most of the battles centered on the areas now occupied by Nicaragua, Guatemala, El Salvador, and Honduras, as Costa Rica and Belize offered few of the riches that the conquerors were seeking. With the added advantage of horses and firearms, the Europeans had conquered all these territories before 1530, at the expense of an enormous loss of Indian lives.

The two principal aims behind the Spanish Conquest of the New World were the search for gold, silver, and other precious metals and the desire to convert the local population to Christianity. Priests and missionaries, including Franciscans and Dominicans, accompanied the invading armies. Other orders followed, including the highly influential Jesuits. During the colonial years, the church grew to be wealthy and powerful by acquiring vast estates of land, and many magnificent cathedrals and churches were constructed.

Colonies of Spain

As the conquerors soon discovered, Central America had little mineral wealth, particularly when compared to the huge fortunes extracted

The Spaniards intended the Cathedral of Santiago de Guatemala to be the grandest building in Central America. For a short time it was, and then on July 29, 1773, a violent earthquake destroyed the city and ruined the cathedral. The building has been left unrepaired in the center of Antigua Guatemala.

from the mountains of Mexico and from the Andes of Bolivia and Peru in South America. There was some gold in Nicaragua. In Honduras, where the highland capital, Tegucigalpa, bears an Indian name meaning "silver hill," the mines were exhausted by the middle of the sixteenth century.

For most of the colonial period Spain had little interest in the Central American colonies. For administrative purposes, most of the territory became part of the Viceroyalty of New Spain, centered in Mexico. However, there was an *audiencia*, a form of council, based in Antigua Guatemala. With a magnificent cathedral, university, and printing press, it was the finest colonial city in the region until it was destroyed by a massive earthquake in 1773. Panama, which was considered to be both culturally and geographically close to South America, became part of the Viceroyalty of Peru.

The Spaniards who did settle took the best of the land, bringing with them grain and cattle from Europe. Several local products were exported back to Spain, including tobacco, cotton, cacao, leather, and wood, but the monarchy enforced heavy taxes on the trade. The most serious consequence of Spanish colonial

---

Bartolomé de Las Casas

After the Spanish Conquest, the Indians of the New World were treated very harshly. By a system known as *encomienda*, the Spanish monarchy allowed the settlers to use the Indians as a labor force, and in return the settlers, or *encomenderos*, were supposed to civilize the Indians. In reality the native peoples became slaves either on the land or in the mines.

One man, the great Dominican priest Bartolomé de Las Casas, fought to defend the rights of the Indians. Himself a former encomendero, he spent the last thirty years of his life, until his death in 1566, pointing out the abuses that were taking place in the New World. He campaigned relentlessly with letters, reports, and sometimes in person to the Spanish king. He was bitterly opposed by other colonists, but it was largely due to his efforts that in 1542 the king issued the New Laws of the Indies. These laws lessened the power of the encomenderos and sought to give some protection to the Indians.

rule was the death of huge numbers of Indians as the result of slavery, enforced labor on the land, and disease. Thousands of Indians were deported to work in the mines in other Spanish colonies, where they worked underground in terrible conditions from which most never returned. Those enslaved by the landowners fared little better. But it was diseases such as influenza and measles, brought by the Europeans and to which the Indians had no immunity, that had the most devastating effect. Marriage between Spanish settlers and the Indians also

Central America had little of the gold and silver the Spaniards were seeking, but tropical forests covering large areas of Central America were a source of hardwoods, which were very valuable in Europe. Some of the remaining forests have been set aside as national parks or reserves and are still rich with valuable hardwoods.

played a part, producing a new mixed race or *mestizo* population, thus generally reducing the pure Indian population.

In the seventeenth century, some European powers, notably the British, took advantage of Spain's disinterest and established settlements along the Caribbean coast in Belize. The forests were full of valuable hardwoods, particularly mahogany, which was in great demand for the making of furniture in Europe. There were good profits to be made. Carib Indians and African slaves from the Caribbean islands were brought in to work in the forests, and they soon outnumbered the settlers. Spain, now aware of the potential of the wood trade, fought back, but it was never able to regain the colony of Belize from the British.

Pirates

All the silver and other treasure taken from the Andes was sent back to Spain through Panama City. From Panama City a rough track crossed to the Caribbean coast, first to the bay of Nombre de Dios and in later years to Portobelo. The route, though little more than a path hacked out through jungle, bore the grand name of the *Camino Real* (Royal Road). It became a prime target for adventurers and pirates. Among the most famous were Francis Drake and Henry Morgan. One hundred years separated the two seamen, and the reasons for their attacks were very different. Drake was an adventurer of Elizabethan times, kindly to the natives and his men, and his main aim was only to annoy the Spaniards while seizing some of the treasure.

Morgan was quite the opposite, a ruthless buccaneer who cared little for life or property.

From the time of Drake's first attack in 1572, the Spaniards began to protect the route by building strongholds and forts, although a long stretch of forbidding jungle still remained as Panama City's best protection. A century later Panama City was rich, with fine houses of mahogany and cedar, monasteries, convents, a cathedral, and treasure houses. There was also a huge market in black slaves, many of them employed as pearl divers off the coast.

In 1671 Henry Morgan assembled a huge fleet with 2,000 men off the Caribbean coast. He was already well acquainted with the Bay Islands of Honduras, which he used as a base to attack the treasure-filled Spanish galleons. However, on this occasion his objective was no less than Panama City itself. It proved a most arduous expedition. The Spaniards, who knew the fleet was coming, retaliated, particularly at Fort San Lorenzo on the Chagres River, and many men were killed or wounded. The exhausted buccaneers also had no food because villages along the way had been evacuated, and the men were too frightened to go hunting in the jungle. The battle for Panama City was short but bloody and ended with the city being burned to the ground, and with it much of the treasure that Morgan sought. Even so, he returned to the Caribbean with some 195 mules loaded with plundered treasure.

Panama City was rebuilt two years later on a new site and attacks on the region continued into the eighteenth century. The British captured Fort

San Lorenzo in 1739 and Portobelo in the following year, after which the Spaniards sent their treasure to Europe around Cape Horn rather than across the isthmus.

Independence from Spain

By the beginning of the nineteenth century many of the Spanish colonies resented the power Spain held over their lands, and a number of local patriots rallied support for independence. Among them were two priests from El Salvador, José Matías Delgado and Manuel José Arce, but their rebellion was crushed. The Central American colonies were too poor and too harshly controlled to take decisive action, and it was not until 1821 when Agustín de Iturbide declared Mexico's independence from Spain that Guatemala, El Salvador, Honduras, Nicaragua, and Costa Rica followed his example.

Iturbide invited these colonies to join his empire, and the decision to accept was made in Guatemala City in 1822. However, some groups of people, and particularly Salvadorans led by Arce and Delgado, were opposed to this decision. Iturbide, now ruling as Emperor Agustín I, tried to enforce his rule but was unsuccessful. Most groups turned against him, and in 1823 a military revolt drove Iturbide from power, leaving the Central American colonies in a position to declare themselves free of Spain. Guatemala, El Salvador, Honduras, Nicaragua, and Costa Rica formed the federation of the United Provinces of Central America.

3   Modern Republics

The federation of the United Provinces of Central America faced many difficulties largely because the countries were poorly prepared for self-government. The basic problem was the opposing views of the conservatives, who represented both the wealthy landowning families and the church, and the liberals, who were more sympathetic to the needs of the common people.

The first president of the federation was the liberal Salvadoran Manuel José Arce. One of his first acts was to abolish slavery, which did not please the conservatives. To make sure they stayed in power, the liberals in 1828, led by General Francisco Morazán, expelled many conservative leaders and took away property from the church. In 1830 Morazán became president, and although he alone decided how things were run, he encouraged reforms in education, trade, and industry and welcomed immigrants.

In the late 1830s, the federation plunged into further conflict with an Indian and mestizo uprising led by archconservative Rafael Carrera. In 1838 the federation congress agreed to let each country choose its own form of government. The federation would have collapsed then if Morazán, first as president of El Salvador in 1838 and then as president of Costa Rica in 1842, had not tried to keep the idea alive. He was eventually defeated, and then shot. With him died all hope for the federation.

Independent states

During the nineteenth century and into the twentieth, the peoples of El Salvador, Guatemala, Nicaragua, and Honduras lived through years of chaos, the breakdown of law and order, dictatorships, assassinations, civil war, and wars among themselves. Most attempts at fair and lawful government or social and economic reform made little impact, and several efforts to bind one or more countries into a group that could work together failed. Conservatives and liberals continued to oppose each other, and the wide gap between rich and poor remained.

Some leaders in this century have introduced limited reforms to give workers more rights and to distribute land to the poor. Their efforts have been hindered by the wealthy conservative

For many years life in Nicaragua has been hard for almost everyone, and survival has often depended on the strength of family life.

classes, and by U.S.–backed foreign firms who own land and run businesses in the region. The United States, fearful of Communist influences, has lent support to domineering and often repressive leaders. Repression has been countered by left-wing guerrilla movements. Right-wing (conservative) death squads have been organized to combat the guerrillas, leading to mass murders, executions, and assassinations. In El Salvador, 75,000 people were killed in 11 years of civil war, and the 1980 assassination of Archbishop Oscar Romero, a champion of the poor, caused worldwide revulsion.

In 1986 and again in 1991 Guatemala held democratic elections, but the army remains the

The Soccer War

El Salvador is the most densely populated country in Central America and has a high rate of unemployment. In the 1950s and 1960s over a quarter of a million people made their way illegally into neighboring Honduras, looking for work. There was considerable ill-feeling between the two countries, partly caused by property law reforms in Honduras that made no provision for the Salvadorans, 15,000 of whom were forced to return to their own country.

Tension between the two countries was at its height when the two national soccer teams were playing each other in qualifying games for the 1969 World Cup. The Salvadoran army launched an attack over the border in Honduras, and the short war that followed, in which 2,000 people were killed, became known as the Soccer War.

real power behind the scene. In El Salvador the extreme-right ARENA party gained control in 1989 and, despite the recent progress in negotiations with the guerrillas, there is only a slim chance for peace. In Honduras, which has had civilian government for ten years, the people are among the poorest in the Western Hemisphere.

After the overthrow of the Somoza family, the National Palace in Managua, Nicaragua, was renamed Palace of the Heroes of the Revolution. Giant paintings of nationalists Augusto César Sandino and Carlos Fonseca now overlook the old square.

Somoza and the Sandinistas

Early in the twentieth century U.S. Marines were stationed in Nicaragua to support successive conservative regimes. The U.S. presence, which lasted almost continuously from 1912 to 1933, was opposed by nationalist forces led by Augusto César Sandino.

37

In 1932 Anastasio Somoza was appointed by the Americans as supreme commander of the Nicaraguan National Guard; two years later Sandino was murdered. In 1936 Somoza declared himself president and began a regime of terror and misery. Somoza was assassinated in 1956 but was succeeded by his two sons, whose governments were as corrupt and ruthless as their father's had been. Little was done for the people, whose plight worsened when the 1972 earthquake devastated their homes. Strikes and demonstrations became commonplace. The brutality of the Somoza regimes attracted worldwide condemnation, and after a long guerrilla war waged by the group now known as the Sandinistas, the Somoza family was overthrown in 1979.

The Government of National Reconstruction, installed by the Sandinistas, inherited a broken country. Thousands had died or been wounded; thousands were jobless and half a million, homeless. The task of rebuilding the ruined economy was formidable. The Sandinistas remained in power until 1990, with Daniel Ortega Saavedra elected president in 1985, but their program for reform encountered many domestic and foreign difficulties. Fearing that the government had Communist leanings, the United States suspended economic aid, imposed a trade embargo, and actively supported an anti-Sandinista group, the Contras, in their attacks against the government.

In 1990 Mrs. Violeta Barrios de Chamorro, widow of a newspaper editor assassinated during the Somoza years, won a surprise victory for the presidency, and her government faced an uphill struggle.

Panama

During the nineteenth century, Panama remained part of the Republic of Colombia. It did not achieve independent status until 1903, an event closely tied to the construction of the Panama Canal. Although a short-cut between oceans had been thought of as early as the sixteenth century, the first route for vehicles across the isthmus was the Panamanian railroad, opened in 1853 to carry Europeans to the gold rush in California, which created the impetus to start the canal.

After successfully completing the Suez Canal, Frenchman Count Ferdinand-Marie de Lesseps arrived in the isthmus in 1881 to construct the canal. Not only were the technical problems different from those in Suez, but the isthmus was very unhealthy. In 8 years, an estimated twenty thousand workers were struck down by tropical diseases. Even so, 19 miles (30 kilometers) had been dug when de Lesseps' company went bankrupt in 1889.

The Colombian Senate first authorized the company to sell its rights and property to the United States, but then changed its mind. The Panamanians took matters into their own hands, and with the support of the United States, declared independence. A deal was struck for the United States to build the canal, and it was given a strip of land 5 miles (8 kilometers) wide on either side of the canal, now known as the Canal Zone, from which to operate it.

Since it was completed in 1914, the Panama Canal has been of major international importance. Today only super tankers and some container ships are too large to pass through it.

The history of Panama since the opening of the canal in 1914 has been dominated by its relationship with the United States. Ownership of the Canal Zone, the most highly developed and populated region in the country, has been a constant source of friction. In 1979 the U.S. Congress authorized the gradual transfer of the canal to Panama, to be completed by the turn of the century.

It remains to be seen whether ownership of the canal will change the fortune of Panama, which for many years has known a depressed economy, unstable government, and corruption. Few incidents better illustrate the state of the nation than the recent arrest, on charges of drug trafficking, of ex-President Noriega, and the

William Crawford Gorgas

The main reason for the French failure to complete the Panama Canal was disease. Thousands of workers died from malaria and yellow fever, which were widespread in the isthmus. By the time the Americans began construction in 1904, it had been discovered that these fevers were spread by mosquitoes. In Cuba an American army doctor, William Crawford Gorgas, had been successful in ridding the city of Havana of yellow fever by identifying and eliminating the disease-carrying mosquito. He was sent to the isthmus with the awesome responsibility of doing the same there.

For a long time he worked under very difficult conditions, without the confidence of many of his superiors and without the right equipment. The turning point came when U.S. President Theodore Roosevelt authorized that Gorgas be given all the assistance he needed. Within months the doctor had cleared the isthmus of yellow fever. He was disappointed that he was unable to completely eradicate malaria, even though he greatly reduced the numbers affected by the disease. Of all the people in authority, Gorgas was the only man to stay in the isthmus throughout the entire period of the construction of the canal. The United States army hospital in Balboa is named in his honor.

failure of the democratic government that followed him to put Panama's house in order.

The peaceful country

Alone among the Central American countries, Costa Rica has had a relatively peaceful and prosperous history since the breakup of the federation. Unable to provide the Spaniards with mineral wealth, the territory was left largely untroubled during the colonial years.

Costa Rica was the first Central American country to cultivate coffee. From an initial trickle of exports, the business flourished until, by 1850, large quantities of coffee were being exported overseas. Costa Rica was also the first Central American country to grow bananas, and the revenue and foreign investment that accompanied the development of its economy laid the foundation for a stable society.

To replace the ox carts used to transport the coffee, the first railroad was built between the Meseta Central and the coast, and roads connected San José and other major towns. Schools were constructed, and in 1886 free public education became compulsory. The church had always been a major influence, but gradually its power was reduced. In 1890 Costa Rica held what is considered to be the first free and honest democratic election in all of Central America, and in 1913 all adults were given the right to vote.

During the twentieth century Costa Rica has managed to retain orderly government despite the strife and chaos of the neighboring countries. Only once have Communists threatened the government, an action that led in 1949 to the abolition of the Costa Rican army and its replacement by civil guard. The man responsible for this legislation, and the republic's leading twentieth-century politician, was José "Don Pepe" Figueres, a farmer-philosopher, founder of one of Costa Rica's main political parties, the

PLN, and twice president of the country.

Economically, in recent years, Costa Rica has experienced the problems of many developing countries: soaring oil prices, heavy international debts, unemployment, and inflation. The PLN government tried to solve these problems, but nonetheless lost the 1990 elections to President Rafael Angel Calderón.

The British colony

By the end of the colonial period, the woodcutters and loggers were well established in Belize. Spain made a final effort to assert its sovereignty over the territory, but the Spaniards, with an army of two thousand five hundred men and thirty ships, were soundly defeated in 1798 by the Belizeans. The British, however, had not claimed the land as a colony. In various treaties with Spain, they had been granted only the right to make use of logwood within specified areas. The trade had become very profitable, and when Mexico and Guatemala achieved independence in 1821, both countries claimed Belize.

Britain and the British settlers rejected these claims, and in 1859 an agreement was signed in which Guatemala relinquished its claim on the condition that Britain contribute to the building of a road from Guatemala City to Belize. The road was never built, and in 1860, when Guatemala threatened to take over the country by military force, the British sent in troops, as few Belizeans wanted to be part of Guatemala. In 1862 Britain declared Belize to be a colony known as British Honduras. Belize was Great Britain's last colony in the Americas.

Coffee, a crop of great value to Costa Rica, is grown successfully on a large, well-organized scale.

During the nineteenth century some attempts were made to widen the range of business by expanding into agricultural products such as bananas, sugar, and citrus fruits. An influx of Spanish-speaking refugees from Mexico added to the small population of Maya Indians, blacks, and Europeans. Although Mexico gave up all claims to the colony in 1893, Guatemala has consistently refused to do so. In 1964 the British government granted rights of self-government to Belize, and in 1981 the colony achieved full independence under the leadership of George Price and the People's United Party. Since then, a British military force has been stationed in Belize to protect the country's borders.

4

The People of Central America

The arrival of the Spaniards and later settlers, slaves, and immigrants in the five hundred years since the conquest has resulted in a population made up of a number of different groups of people. The most numerous are mestizos, or people of mixed blood, a group that originated early after the conquest when marriages took place between Spaniards and Indians.

Descendants of Europeans, mainly Spanish and sometimes known as Creoles, make up the next largest group. Various Indian peoples have survived and in Guatemala account for about half the population, although elsewhere only small scattered groups are found in both the highlands and lowlands. Another group are the blacks, which includes a very few pure-blooded Africans, and a much larger number of mulattoes, or descendants of African and European marriages. Still other groups are the zambos, descendants of black and American-Indian marriages, and black Caribs, also known as Garifuna, who are descendants of Carib Indians and black slaves brought from Africa to the West Indies and from there to Central America. There are also a small number of immigrants from different parts of the world.

The distribution of the various groups is not the same in any one country in Central America. This is largely due to the movements of the Spaniards in their quest for mineral wealth. The Indians in

Guatemala survived because they did well in battle and escaped the ravages of the Europeans by fleeing into the mountains. In El Salvador, Honduras, Nicaragua, and Panama, where Spaniards and Indians mixed, the mestizos make up the majority of the population, while in Costa Rica, uniquely, over 90 percent of the population is of European descent. The blacks, brought in to work first in the forests and later on the banana plantations, are found mainly on the coast of the Caribbean.

A group of Nicaraguan school teachers of mixed race meet in Managua. These mestizos have come from different parts of the country to join a protest for higher salaries.

Mestizos

Mestizos live and work in both towns and the countryside. They form the bulk of the working classes, although there are some wealthy mestizo

landowners and businessmen; there are also very poor mestizos. All forms of work are open to mestizos, depending on their level of education. In the cities and towns they enter the medical and legal professions, or they take up manual work, perhaps in the building or manufacturing industries. Some work independently as taxi drivers, merchants, or servants in wealthier households. Mestizos are also to be found at every level of political life, from president to messenger.

Outside the towns the wealthier mestizos own their own farms, and the less well-off rent or sharecrop the land. Very poor mestizos farm at a subsistence level, growing food only for their own needs; others concentrate on cash crops that they can sell in local markets. To supplement their income, some families specialize in pottery, weaving, and other crafts. Others work in small factories that provide employment in the making

Ladinos
In Central America, and particularly in Guatemala, the word *Ladino* is used to describe Indians who adopt Western dress and customs. Young Indians, without hope of acquiring land on which to grow crops, are often forced by financial pressures to seek work in the towns, and so become Ladinos. The definition is cultural, not racial, but in taking this step Indians often cut themselves off from their own background and people. They are not always welcomed back into the rural community.

of clothes, furniture, tiles, and certain household items. Whether in the tropical lowlands or cooler mountains, mestizos wear Western-style dress and, among the wealthy, part of the life-style is to follow American and European fashion trends.

The "tico" of Costa Rica

The Indian population of the Meseta Central of Costa Rica disappeared almost entirely soon after the Spanish Conquest, mainly because of disease, and there was little intermarriage between Europeans and Indians. As a result, today's population of about three million is predominantly descended from the Spanish settlers who arrived to develop the land. The affectionate nickname "tico" is often used when referring to Costa Ricans, who have a courteous

In Costa Rica these men and boys of largely European descent enjoy horseback riding in a game of skill similar to jousting.

and friendly manner. Tico is from *momentico*, which means "just a little moment" and refers to the small size of the country. At work and at home they live in much the same way as their mestizo neighbors in other countries. However, in appearance, with their paler skin and dress closely modeled on that worn in America, Costa Ricans could be mistaken for residents of any American or European city.

The Indians

The Indians of the highlands of Guatemala are descendants of the Maya and of groups with whom the Maya mixed after the Spanish Conquest. The most important of these groups are the Quiché, the Cakchiquel, the Tzutuhil, the

The market in Chichicastenango is a regular event in the lives of the Indians. They use the occasion to meet, talk, and sell and barter goods.

Mam, and the Kekchi. In El Salvador descendants of the Pipil Indians live in the village of Panchimalco, south of San Salvador.

Indian homes are simple, made from adobe mud brick, bamboo, and wattle or rock, although in many places old thatched roofs of straw or palm have given way to corrugated tin or asbestos shingles. Some Indians own a small piece of land where they grow corn and a few other crops. Some work cooperatively in a village, and others are employed on coffee, fruit, or cotton plantations.

It is in their dress that the Guatemalan Indians are most distinctive, with different styles distinguishing one village from another. Although men have to some extent now adopted Western clothing, the women have remained very traditional and are famous for their weaving artistry. They wear a headdress of ribbons intertwined with long braids that are then wrapped or twisted around the head. Skirts are usually woven lengths of brightly striped cloth wrapped around the waist and held up by embroidered multicolored sashes. Over her

Indian Markets
Indian market days in the highlands, and particularly in the Quiché center of Chichicastenango, create a wonderfully colorful scene. Heaps of richly patterned belts, blankets, masks, clay pots, gourds, and other handicrafts are for sale, alongside flowers, fruit, vegetables, chickens, and other produce brought in by Indian families from the countryside.

shoulders an Indian woman wraps a striped woven cloth of bright colors that she uses to carry her baby or market produce, or to cover her head in church. However, the Indian woman's most attractive and exquisitely decorated garment is her blouse, or *huipil*. She may have several for everyday use and for such occasions as weddings and funerals.

Other small groups of Indians still exist, descendants of tribes who were much less organized than the Maya. Among these are the Bribrí and Cabecar in Costa Rica, where the Indian population now on reserved land numbers no more than 5,000, and a very small number of Paya and Miskito Indians in Honduras. The Miskito, living on the northern Caribbean coast, are also the largest group in Nicaragua. In Panama there are the Guaymí; the Cuna, who live in the Archipelago of San Blas; and the Chocó, in scattered groups in the Darién.

Most of these Indians live as their ancestors did, hunting with bows and arrows and fishing from dug-out canoes, which are made by skillfully hollowing out light wood logs. They grow a few simple crops, such as corn, manioc, and yams, and often keep pigs and chickens.

The Cuna are the most Westernized of Panama's Indians, even having their own representative in the National Assembly, as San Blas is a self-governing territory. Many Cuna now send their children to school in towns and have themselves become involved in town life. Within their homes, it is not unusual to find transistor radios and aluminum pots and pans. Motorboats are gradually replacing traditional canoes. The women wear colorful dress, with cotton appliquéd blouses and wraparound skirts. They wear many decorations, such as necklaces of glass beads, shells, or fish bones, and strings of colored beads around their arms and legs. Many of the women and girls wear a small gold ring in their nose.

The blacks

In the Darién and the Pearl Islands of Panama there are small groups of blacks who can perhaps claim direct African descent, as their ancestors escaped from their Spanish owners and established separate, isolated communities of their own. However, most of the black population cannot be distinguished from other Central

Blacks are in the majority in Belize. These schoolchildren can expect to enjoy a good education.

Americans except by color, as through marriage and with the passage of time they have become culturally and socially absorbed into the society of the country in which they live. There are exceptions, however, including English-speaking blacks on the Caribbean coast of Nicaragua, Honduras, and Costa Rica, who have kept their Protestant religion, and black Caribs, most of whom live on the Honduran coast and the southern coast of Belize.

The black Caribs live mainly by fishing, using harpoons, hooks and line, and sometimes fish traps made locally from reeds. To supplement their diet, they have fields of manioc or cassava, which is a root from which they make small flat

Language
Spanish is the official language in all the republics of Central America except Belize, although Spanish is spoken there also by a large number of the population. English is the first language of Belize, and there are English-speaking blacks, particularly on the Mosquito Coast of Nicaragua and Honduras. In all these regions, a "creole" form of English is also used, which mixes English with French, black Carib, Indian, and Spanish words. Indian languages have survived, particularly in the Mayan area of Guatemala, where an estimated 1.5 million people are thought to speak Quiché, Cakchiquel, Mam, or Kekchi. Miskito, the principal native language in Nicaragua, is also spoken in Honduras, where a small number of other Indian languages are also heard. Native speakers in Panama include the Guaymí, Cuna, and Chocó Indians, relatively few of whom speak Spanish.

cakes. In recent years many men have had to leave their families and villages to seek work elsewhere, yet the black Caribs have kept their own separate identity and some of their traditional ceremonies. In Belize their national festival takes place annually in November in the town of Dangriga on what is known as Carib Settlement (or Garifuna) Day.

The immigrants
There have not been mass movements of immigrants from Europe and elsewhere to Central America as in other parts of Latin America. During the nineteenth century, however, some groups of foreigners were imported or arrived of their own free will to undertake work for which the small local population was unsuited. From China cheaply-hired, unskilled laborers were brought in to help build the Panamanian railroad alongside some French and U.S. nationals. During the construction of the Panama Canal more Americans arrived, as well as Jamaicans, Spaniards, Italians, and Greeks.

Other immigrants arrived in Central America to trade, notably more Chinese, who are present today in Guatemala, Belize, Honduras, and Panama, and Arabs from Syria and Lebanon. Hindus and Jews are also involved in commerce and industry. Small numbers of educated European immigrants include Spanish, Italian, Scots, Irish, and Germans, and more recently religious communities such as Mennonites and Quakers. A growing number of Americans, many in retirement, are now living in several of the Central American countries.

5 Daily Life

Many of the major cities of Central America were founded by the Spaniards, but three of these cities became capitals only in the nineteenth century: San José in 1823, Managua in 1858, and Tegucigalpa in 1880. Of the capitals, Guatemala City, San José, Tegucigalpa, and San Salvador are in the highlands. Belize City is built on a swamp at sea level, and Managua is in the hot lowlands on the edge of Lake Managua. The strategic importance of Panama City on the Pacific side of the canal has never been in doubt. It was founded in 1673 after Henry Morgan had sacked the old

Belmopan

After Hurricane Hattie devastated Belize City in 1961, construction was begun on a new capital, Belmopan, some 50 miles (80 km) inland. Today Belmopan is Belize's administrative capital and seat of government. It has a National Assembly building, government office buildings, and housing for civil servants. Many people, however, continue to live on the coast and make the hour-long journey to work each day. Belmopan is well connected by a major road, the Western Highway, to Belize, and by the same highway to the frontier with Guatemala. Belmopan also stands at the junction of the Western Highway with the scenically attractive Hummingbird Highway, which leads to the Maya Mountains and the town of Dangriga. Belmopan is well situated, but much has to be done to complete the construction of the new city.

town. It is significant that Panama's second city, Colón, is sited on the Atlantic side of the canal.

Other important cities include Santa Ana, the second-largest city in El Salvador, located on the slopes of the volcano from which it takes its name; Quetzaltenango, set among high volcanoes in western Guatemala; and the industrial center of San Pedro, the fastest-growing city in Central America, in the northern lowlands of Honduras.

In an endless succession of floods, hurricanes, earthquakes, and wars, disaster has hit most of these cities at some time and destroyed many of the original colonial buildings. Office buildings and houses are now built with disasters in mind. In flood areas homes are erected on stilts, and in

American culture is everywhere in evidence in Costa Rica. The center of San José boasts fast-food restaurants and mounted tourist police.

city centers there are only a small number of skyscrapers and many one-story buildings. Managua, in particular, suffered badly with the combined devastation of the 1972 earthquake and the long revolutionary war, which ended in 1979. An important part of the Sandinista program was to build housing developments for the thousands who were homeless.

For the poorer people in the cities, homes are built of wood or brick with tin roofs, often lack electricity and running water, and have open drains instead of proper sanitation. There are fewer shanty towns in Nicaragua than in many parts of Latin America, as in Nicaragua there has been a significant reduction in the movement of people from rural areas. There are also well-

Low-cost housing built in Managua after the earthquake was essential for a needy population.

planned residential areas, with large houses and gardens full of tropical plants, well-lit streets, established parks, markets for traditional handicrafts and fruits and vegetables, and modern shopping centers, where American-style fast-food stands are very popular. In Belize City, where American influence is also felt, the clapboard houses, white-painted timber mansions, and main streets named Regent Street and Albert Street give the appearance of a British colonial town.

Living in the countryside

With the exception of El Salvador, the density of population per square mile in Central America is low. In all countries 40 percent or more live in the cities and towns. The remaining rural population is scattered in villages where basic facilities are very limited and sometimes nonexistent. People build their houses from whatever local materials are available, usually slatted wood or mud brick, with tin or corrugated-iron roofs. Furniture is simple and mostly homemade, perhaps with the addition of a few plastic chairs, and in the lowlands no home is without a hammock.

In fertile highland regions homes and villages are often surrounded by well-cultivated fields, with crops of corn, beans, rice, vegetables, and fruit, farmed by families who can afford fertilizers, irrigation, and maybe a tractor. However, many subsistence farmers, with little more than bare hands and some basic tools, can barely scrape a living from the land and are lucky to find other jobs like cutting timber or working on a plantation to supplement their income. If

In the Petén of Guatemala the people, who are mostly subsistence farmers, build very simple homes using local materials from the surrounding tropical forest.

there is no work, families keep themselves busy by sewing or making baskets and other handicrafts to sell in the towns. In the humid coastal lowlands, where people are employed on the sugar and banana plantations, the work is hard and tiring. As compensation many fruit companies provide small clapboard or corrugated-iron homes for the workers, and sometimes schools, medical facilities, and even movie theaters.

On the Mosquito Coast and in the Bay Islands off Honduras and the cays of Belize, people work as fishermen, boatbuilders, in the coconut trade, or in some aspect of tourism. Their life is very relaxed, and no one worries if work stops for a game of cards or to play music.

Family life

The strong family unit that is traditional in Central America, and especially in rural communities, is essential if people are to survive the extreme hardships brought on by war and natural disasters. It is customary for several generations to live together, and everyone, from young children to grandparents, contributes to the family's survival. This support network has become even more necessary as the men of the family increasingly move away to find work in the towns or more prosperous areas, or join the fighting groups of guerrillas, or themselves become targets of murderous death squads.

The burden of raising the family has fallen heavily on the shoulders of the women in recent years. In addition to domestic chores and using any spare time to make handicrafts, they must now look after the crops and animals. Those who live in the towns must seek some kind of employment. At an early age children are expected to help, either by looking after younger brothers and sisters or by earning small sums of money in the streets, perhaps by shining shoes, selling trinkets, or washing cars.

Families also help each other through a relationship known as *compradrazgo*, which is a formal tie of mutual respect between the godfather, or sponsor at baptism, and father of a child. The godfather plays an active part in bringing up his godson or goddaughter. He will attend all important family occasions and, if it becomes necessary, he will take over the role of father. It is his duty to see that the child is brought up and disciplined properly.

For many people lunch is a simple meal. Beside the Palace of the Heroes of the Revolution in Managua, an outdoor kitchen provides inexpensive meals of fried plantains, pork, and chicken.

Food

The basic foods for country-dwellers and many townspeople throughout Central America are corn, rice, and beans, prepared in a variety of ways. The most common dishes are *tortillas*, or corn pancakes that can be filled with different meats, beans, or cheese. A version of these are *pupusas*, sometimes served as snacks. *Baleadas* are soft flour tortillas filled with beans and various combinations of butter, eggs, cheese, and cabbage. Another favorite dish is *tamales*, made of corn dough with a mixture of fillings, including rice, tomatoes, chilis, potatoes, and meat, all wrapped in a large banana leaf. Corn is also the basis for an alcoholic drink called *chicha*, which is particularly popular at fiesta time. Black beans are

61

an important part of the diet. They are an important source of protein for those who cannot afford to buy meat and fish.

Fish are plentiful on the coast, however, and are served as a stew with bananas and coconut milk. In Panama, which is famous for its lobsters, shrimp, tuna, and other seafood, a dish called *seviche*, made of raw whitefish marinated in lemon or lime, is common. A wide variety of vegetables, meat, beans, chicken, and even eggs are used in stews and soups. These, like many dishes, are often spiced with hot peppers. Fruit is plentiful in many places, and coconuts are an important ingredient in puddings, cakes, fish dishes, or as plain coconut rice.

Although many of these foods are grown locally, at times there are severe shortages and widespread malnutrition. In the cities, for the wealthier families, there are cosmopolitan restaurants, and in San José and Panama City, where American influence is greatest, hot dogs and hamburgers are now part of the way of life.

Religion

As a result of the Spanish Conquest, the majority of the population of Central America is Roman Catholic, although people are free to practice any religion. Other denominations include Baptists, Methodists, Mormons, and also Episcopalians, particularly in Belize. The Mennonites in Belize and Quakers in Costa Rica are now well established, and non-Catholic missionaries work in many countries. Tragically, they are sometimes caught in the crossfire between guerrillas and armies, even though they normally do not get involved in politics. Much to the disapproval of the pope as head of the Roman Catholic Church, some priests became involved in supporting the Sandinistas against the Somozas and continued to play an important role once the Sandinistas were in power. Religious services are well attended, and churches remain open all day so that people may pray, light candles, or just meditate whenever they wish. Families, however poor, celebrate baptisms, confirmations, and other important religious occasions in the traditional way.

Although nominally Catholic, the Indian people still cling to their traditional beliefs. They worship their gods of the mountains, valleys, rivers, corn, and rain whom they believe will influence their daily lives. They place stone idols, carved images of their gods, and wooden crosses on the tops of mountains. Every week in Chichicastenango in Guatemala, Indians ceremoniously fill the Church of Santo Tomás with candles and incense before presenting offerings of flower petals and candles made from an aromatic resin called copal to the *idolo*, a black image of a Maya god set on a nearby hilltop. Easter Week in Chichicastenango is also very colorful as the Indians, observing the Catholic ritual, make a grand procession through the streets, carrying a huge cross and statues of Christ and the saints. Bright carpets, made of dyed sawdust and flowers, are laid on the route, and only the litter bearing Christ and His cross are allowed to pass over them.

6   Education, Health, and Leisure

These schoolchildren in Managua are carrying their desks from one classroom to another nearby. Nicaragua has been running a campaign to improve the education of the population and, as in other Central American countries, school is compulsory beginning at age six.

Many people in Central America still cannot read or write. The rate of illiteracy differs from one country to another, but is lowest in Belize and in Costa Rica, which has benefited from its long-established educational system. Illiteracy is highest in El Salvador and Guatemala. Nicaragua has lowered its illiteracy rate drastically by a campaign organized by the Sandinistas that began in 1980, the "Year of Literacy." At that time about half the population was illiterate. Under the direction of a Catholic priest and poet, Father Fernando Cardenal, teachers were trained, books were printed, and thousands of volunteers were sent from the towns to teach the country people to read and write. The illiteracy rate is now below 10 percent.

In most countries education is officially free and compulsory from about the ages of six to fifteen, with an emphasis on the primary years. In reality it is impossible to enforce such legislation because there are too few qualified teachers, insufficient funds, and in many rural areas either badly equipped schools or no schools at all. To reach a rural school, many children have to walk several miles each day, taking with them any food they need. Children go to school only if their parents allow them to do so, and parents often keep young members of the family at home to work on the land.

Some parents who want their children to be educated move into the towns and cities where the best private and public schools, colleges, and universities are found. Many of these are run by the Roman Catholic Church. In school, apart from learning the basic skills of reading and writing, children study arts and science subjects similar to those in American and European schools. At a higher level there are opportunities to take vocational training or to qualify for professional work.

Health
Life expectancy in Central America is considerably shorter than in developed countries, and there is a high mortality rate

After many troubled years, some parts of Managua are still without proper drainage. This open ditch carries waste to Lake Managua.

among young babies. The climate encourages the spread of disease, and poor living conditions make things worse. Since the construction of the Panama Canal and the work done by the American William Crawford Gorgas, many tropical diseases have been eliminated or controlled within the Central American countries. Yet people are still at risk from malaria and dengue fever, occasional outbreaks of yellow fever, and most of all from diseases such as typhoid and gastroenteritis, which are caused by contaminated water. Water supplies, even in the cities, are often inadequate, and damage incurred by earthquakes and guerrilla attacks greatly increases the risk of disease. In poor areas families often have to collect their water from standpipes, and many homes are surrounded by open sewers. Malnutrition is another problem. Not only is food sometimes in short supply, but many rural people do not understand the need for a balanced diet.

When the Sandinistas came to power in Nicaragua, health care was one of the first problems they tried to solve. Doctors and nurses were sent into the countryside to communities that previously had never received medical help.

Without access to modern medicines, some rural people rely on their own traditional methods for treating illness. Even today many are reluctant to change their ways. They are superstitious, believing disease stems from natural causes such as the weather. They resort to *curanderos*, or curers, who may use herbs and

Herbal medicines have been used by many generations of people in Central America. Natural products from the forests are sold at local markets, often with a clear description of the ailment to be cured.

secret remedies, as well as some modern medicines. In the markets, stands with shelves filled with herbal and natural remedies, each well labeled, are sought by many people. The best hospitals and clinics are concentrated in the towns and cities and are publicly and privately run. In several countries, particularly in Costa Rica where a social welfare system has been in operation for many years, workers can receive free treatment. The hospitals, however, have a difficult task maintaining standards because funds are not always available for medicines and modern equipment.

Leisure

As in many South American and European countries, soccer is the national sport in most Central American countries, except in Nicaragua, which shares the North American love of baseball. Both games are enjoyed by every sector of the population, either as supporters of national teams, which compete in stadiums in the towns and cities, or as participants, by kicking a ball around with a group of friends in the street or on an open field. Horse racing also attracts crowds, and there are facilities for competitive and organized sports such as golf, sailing, and tennis, but only a few people can afford these more expensive pastimes.

For the majority of working people, who are less well-off and have little time for relaxation, entertainment is provided by television or a visit to the movies, where there is always a choice of internationally made films. Outside the towns, people like to picnic and walk in the mountains,

Costa Rican schoolchildren play basketball in a school playground in San José.

and vacation homes for the wealthy and the international community are increasing in number near places like Lake Atitlán. Swimming and diving are popular on the Caribbean coast, and there are plenty of opportunities for sea and freshwater fishing.

Some traditional entertainments have survived since colonial times, such as horseback riding, cockfighting, and bullfighting, although the bull is seldom killed. These events often take place during local fiestas, which are particularly enjoyed by people in rural communities.

7 A Cultural Tradition

Archaeologists have found a wealth of material that demonstrates the richness of Mayan artistry, not only in the architecture of huge pyramids and palaces or in the elaborately carved stelae with their representations of gods and daily life, but also in sculpture, pottery, stucco work, and painting. Sculptures are of stone and found mostly in the temples where they were intended only for the gods to see. Often stylized, they are elaborate in their detail. Artisans worked with great care, as any mistake led to severe punishment. The Mayan potters were women. With no knowledge of the potter's wheel and with kilns fired with wood or charcoal, they produced a huge variety of vessels for both domestic and ceremonial use. Some of the finest examples are incense burners and urns for the ashes of the dead, often decorated with grotesque faces. The potters also made ceramic figures of humans and animals.

Stucco work is the art of modeling in a form of plaster applied to buildings, sculptures, and pottery. It was widely used by the Maya, who also lavishly painted many of the things they made in a range of colors, including black, red, orange, and gray. Some murals, or wall paintings, have also been discovered, although these too were originally intended to be seen only by the gods. In particularly good condition are some paintings recently discovered lining a tomb in Río Azul in Guatemala.

The Maya also worked in jade, which is a very

A funerary urn from the Guatemalan highlands made by the Quiché-Maya about 1,200 years ago. The curious faces represent spirits to guard the remains of the deceased.

hard stone, and they produced ornaments, jewelry for the nobles, and pendants in the shape of an ax that are known as Ax-Gods. Magnificent jade heads have been found in tombs in Guatemala, one weighing over 12 pounds (5.5 kilograms), and in Altun Ha in Belize. Gold, although known to the Maya, originated mostly from Panama, where styles were influenced by South American civilizations. Many effigy pendants represent jaguars and other animals, or bird heads on human bodies.

Indian arts

The Indian weavings of Guatemala are the finest in Central America and rank among the finest in the world. Weaving is not just a practical necessity to the Indian way of life, but a deep-rooted part of their cultural tradition. Changes have taken place since the Spanish Conquest, particularly in the use of materials, but despite the pressures of modern living, Indian women often turn to their looms whenever they have a spare moment.

Due to the humid tropical conditions, the work of Mayan weavers has not survived. They used cotton and took their dyes from natural plants

Each region of Guatemala is known for a different style of weaving. The Quiché weaving from the northern highlands is among the most distinctive and is sold in the markets.

and minerals. Black was extracted from coal, yellow from the blackberry trees, red from the seeds of the *achiote* plant, and blue from clay. The most difficult color to obtain was purple, as this was taken from cochineals, insects that live on cactus. Today synthetic materials and dyes are used as well as cotton and wool.

Mayan weavers used back-strap looms much as the Indian women do now for their huipils. The loom has two wooden rods, securing the warp at top and bottom, with one end secured to a pole or tree and the other attached to the weaver's waist. Foot looms, introduced by the Spaniards, are also used but only by the men, to make larger, commercial pieces of cloth such as the wrap-around skirts.

Designs used by the Cuna Indians for their cotton appliqué-worked molas have been passed down through the family. Many of the colorful patterns originated in the spiritual visions of ancestors.

Highly decorated ox carts are one of Costa Rica's great traditions, but the craft has died out in all but a few places. The annual festival in San Antonio de Escazu, where the carts and drivers gather, draws large crowds from the capital, San José.

It can take Indian women many months to make a huipil, incorporating different designs and vibrant colors. Many of the motifs have a significance steeped in Mayan history and related to the natural world. Animals, birds, flowers, and the sun and moon are all popular designs worked into the cloth, and central to Mayan beliefs is the diamond-shaped pattern that represents the four corners of the Mayan world.

Motifs and designs representing the animal and plant world are also features of colorful appliqué work done by the Cuna Indians of Panama, which they incorporate into blouses and baskets. Some Cuna women still weave their own hammocks of homespun cotton on vertical looms. Other handicrafts from Central America include simple pots and water jars, decorated gourds, wooden and ceramic ornaments, and macramé (knotted thread) articles.

Art and literature

Of all the Central American countries, Guatemala has the strongest artistic tradition, beginning with the hieroglyphic writing of the Maya, and *Popol Vuh*, the sacred book of the Quiché-Maya that relates the tribe's creation myths and was written after the arrival of the Spaniards. During colonial times, the Spaniards built many fine churches and cathedrals. There is a large, splendid cathedral in León, Nicaragua, that is said to have been built by mistake, when plans for a cathedral in the important colonial city of Lima in Peru got mixed up with those for a modest church in León. In Panama's cathedral is the magnificent gold altar that was successfully hidden from the pirate Henry Morgan. The Spaniards lavished the most attention on Antigua Guatemala, the most important city in the region. Many of the buildings have since been destroyed in earthquakes, but the elaborate baroque-style cathedral and a number of the civic buildings are still standing.

In modern times Central America's most acclaimed writer and artist have both come from Guatemala. Writer Miguel Angel Asturias (1899–1974), like many of his Latin-American contemporaries, related his works to events and peoples of his native land. In a desire to understand the mind of the Indian peoples, he turned to Mayan tradition and particularly *Popol Vuh*, which he translated, and which helped him produce his masterpiece, *Maize Men*. Among his other powerful novels are *Mr. President* and *Mulatto Woman*. In 1967 he was awarded the Nobel Prize for literature.

Mural painting has become a tradition in parts of Central America, and often the art is heavily influenced by political affairs. This painting covers the walls of a library in Managua.

A contemporary of Angel Asturias, the artist Carlos Mérida was born in Quetzaltenango of Quiché-Maya descent. He too looked to indigenous folklore, native crafts, and pre-Columbian cultures to establish a true "American art," and in his early years he completed the series *Images of Guatemala*. After 1950 he turned to architectural art. His work culminated in a gigantic mosaic mural for the Municipal Building in Guatemala City called *The Mestizo Race of Guatemala*.

In recent years a number of artists have continued to concentrate on Guatemalan subjects in their paintings and sculptures. Many have achieved international acclaim, such as Roberto Ossaye, Rodolfo Abularach, and the sculptor

Roberto Goyri. For some of the younger generation, it is difficult to work in the political conditions of Guatemala, and yet, for the artist Alfredo Ceibal, now living in New York, the focus of his magical paintings still lies in Guatemala.

One man who did not come from Guatemala, and who had a profound influence on literature at the turn of the twentieth century, was the Nicaraguan Rubén Darío (1867–1916). Darío was an internationally influential poet whose name is associated with the movement known as *modernismo*, which he initiated with his book *Azul* in 1888. Today another of Central America's leading poets is the priest Ernesto Cardenal, who was responsible for the Sandinista's literacy campaign.

Music, dance, and fiestas

Spanish, African, Caribbean, and Indian influences are all present in Central American music and dance. The Spaniards introduced stringed instruments such as the guitar, mandolin, and violin. From the African and Caribbean cultures have come steel bands, rhythm and reggae, and the marimba, an instrument that resembles a large xylophone but is made of special wood. Indian folklore is an integral part of many colorful fiestas, with the theme of dances often dating from Spanish colonial times. Granada, in Nicaragua, is famous for its Indian dances, such as the *Baile de los Diabolitos* (Dance of the Little Devils), in which "devils" perform in brilliant costumes, devil masks, and Indian headdresses. In Chichicastenango, in celebration of St. Thomas's

Day just before Christmas, the Dance of the Conquest is performed by Indians representing the two sides, with the Spaniards and Indians distinguished by wooden masks and colorful costumes. During these festivities a "flying pole" over 60 feet (18 meters) high is erected in front of the Church of Santo Tomás, from which two men attached to long ropes "fly" to the ground.

Most fiestas are related to important dates in the Catholic calendar, particularly Easter Week and pre-Lent Carnival. The four days of Carnival in Panama City are very colorful, with women in their traditional *pollera* dress, full-skirted and prettily embroidered, and with satin slippers and pearl hair ornaments. Men wear *montuno* outfits of straw hats and embroidered blouses.

Several countries have national dances, including the *punto guanacateco* from the Guanacaste province of Costa Rica, and the *tamborito* of Panama, which is accompanied by three kinds of regional drums. Other popular dances are the *cumbia* of African origin, the merengue, waltz, tango, and bolero, and modern dances from other parts of the world.

8   Across the Isthmus

In 1928 construction was begun on the Pan-American Highway, a road designed to run from North America through Mexico and the Central American republics to South America. Today the highway is complete, except for the section through the jungles of the Darién. The only country through which it does not pass is Belize. The highway connects the capital cities of Guatemala, El Salvador, Nicaragua, Costa Rica, and Panama, with a branch road to Tegucigalpa in Honduras. Belize City can be reached by a series of connections on small roads. The highway runs down the western side of Central America, crossing mountains and winding through valleys, and for most of the route it is paved or has a good all-weather surface. The highway is used frequently by international buses carrying passengers on scheduled routes between the capital cities and by commercial trucks and other vehicles.

But elsewhere in Central America many roads are poor, some little more than dirt tracks that become impassable in the rainy season. Another hazard is volcanic ash, which makes the unpaved roads dusty in the dry season and muddy in the wet season. Maintaining the roads in good condition is also difficult because earthquakes, hurricanes, and guerrilla attacks have caused considerable damage that is costly to repair.

El Salvador is considered to have the best road network, Belize the worst. In Panama a paved highway now crosses the isthmus, connecting

Roads are often damaged by earthquakes. In Costa Rica the Pan-American Highway had to be repaired after a strong tremor shook the region.

Panama City to Colón, and in 1955 the Thatcher Ferry Bridge was built between Panama City and Balboa, which is on the opposite side of the Panama Canal.

Buses, or trucks that have been converted to buses, filled to capacity with people and bundles, are widely used in the cities and in the country. In several cities, huge ex-school buses, imported from the United States and still painted yellow, are commonly used for public transportation. Belize City, especially, seems to have become a graveyard for enormous "gas guzzlers," as the big American cars of the 1950s and 1960s were called because of the large amounts of fuel they used. Many country people still use mules and ox carts as a means of transportation.

Any form of public transportation becomes very crowded. Here people crowd into a jeep that serves as a taxi.

The Panama Canal

The Panama Canal was and is a remarkable engineering achievement. Although canals had been built elsewhere, none had ever faced such enormous problems. The major technical difficulty was a difference in altitude of about 86 feet (26 meters) between parts of the isthmus and the two oceans. The solution was a system of locks that raise and lower as ships pass through the canal. This entailed digging a ditch through a mountain range, wide and deep enough to float oceangoing ships, and constructing the largest dam and the most massive canal locks and gates ever built. New electrical and mechanical devices were invented to operate the waterway, and all the work was carried out despite the constant

A system of gigantic locks is the key to the working of the Panama Canal. Oceangoing vessels have to be lifted 86 feet (26 meters) between the Atlantic side and the Pacific Ocean.

threat of landslides and widespread disease.

Today some 42 ships pass through the canal daily and take between 8 and 9 hours to complete the journey. Six miles (10 kilometers) upriver from the Atlantic is the Gatún dam, beyond which ships ascend 86 feet (26 meters) through three locks to Lake Gatún, whose waters serve to fill the locks. Each lock is 1,000 feet (303 meters) long, and the huge gates are opened to allow water to flow into the lower lock, raising the level to the level of the lock above. All but the smallest ships are then towed through the locks by electric locomotives called "mules." The operation requires an enormous amount of water. An estimated 52 million gallons are lost each time a ship passes through the canal, and it is possible only because of the heavy rainfall in Panama and the construction of a high-level reservoir, the Madden Dam.

Emerging from Lake Gatún, ships steam through the Gaillard or Culebra Cut—the Big Ditch—to the Pedro Miguel Locks, where the descent to sea level is begun. Ships first pass through Miraflores Lake, 56 feet (17 meters) above sea level, and then are lowered in two steps at the Miraflores Locks and finally pass through the canal channel under the Thatcher Ferry Bridge to the Pacific Ocean.

Many international shipping lines call into other ports in Central America, such as Puerto Limón in Costa Rica, Santo Tomás de Castilla in Guatemala, Bluefields in Nicaragua, and Puerto Cortés in Honduras, on the Atlantic coast. The Pacific ports tend to be less important because the open sea makes docking more difficult and ships have to anchor offshore. Belize City, the main port of Belize, has no docks or deep-water quays.

Railroads
Of the few railroads in Central America, most were built by the banana and fruit companies to carry freight. One of the first lines was

Nicaraguan trains are infrequent and always crowded, but they provide an essential and inexpensive link between some towns.

constructed between Cartago and Puerto Limón in Costa Rica by an American, Minor C. Keith, who made a fortune from the banana business. Still one of the most enjoyable journeys in Central America, it passes through the narrow, wooded Reventazón Valley and along the seashore, but the construction of the last 25 miles (40 kilometers) of track in the 1870s cost the lives of 4,000 workers and engineers.

Several railroad lines connect the east and west coasts of Central America. The shortest is the 49-mile (79-kilometer) Panama-Colón railroad, completed in 1855. In Costa Rica an extension of the Puerto Limón to Cartago line reaches Puntarenas on the Pacific coast, and in Guatemala a line runs between Puerto Barrios on the Atlantic coast and the Pacific port of San José. By using part of the Guatemalan railroad network, El Salvador also has a rail route from the Pacific coast through to the Atlantic.

Most people in the republics, however, prefer to travel by road, as the passenger railroads have old-fashioned cars and are usually without any refreshment facilities. The condition of the track and cars is poor, and service is often canceled, particularly in the wet season when the tracks are flooded.

By air

All the Central-American republics have domestic airlines that connect the major towns within each country. There are also national airlines that have scheduled routes to the capital cities of Central America and internationally to Mexico, South America, the United States, and Canada.

Foreign airlines also make regular flights to the capital cities, all of which have international airports. Cuscatlán Airport, serving San Salvador, is the largest and most modern, but air traffic is heaviest in Panama. Not only are there more than 100 airports, but Panama's unique position makes it an ideal connecting point for airlines with routes all over North and South America.

The media

News reaches people even in the remote regions of Central America through the many radio stations. Some are state-owned, some private, and some are no more than one person playing records or cassettes of *musica ranchera*, the popular local brassy music, with frequent

Public telephones in San José are new and well maintained. The telecommunications revolution has brought direct dialing throughout most of Central America.

interruptions for advertisements. Radio stations have also been put to good use by religious and educational organizations who transmit more informative programs.

Television is not as widespread as radio, but commercial and educational stations are reaching an increasingly large audience. The most popular programs are soap operas, or *novelas*, and locally broadcast films produced in the United States and Mexico. Some countries can also receive programs directly from the United States by satellite, and in the area of the Canal Zone in Panama, U.S. armed forces radio and television stations broadcast a variety of programs in English.

9 Business and Trade

The countries of Central America share with most developing countries the overriding burden of huge international debts. Today the Central American economy can be sustained only with the help of international loans and very considerable aid from the United States.

Financial aid has often been decided by political events and U.S. approval of the government in power. Honduras has been well supported because of its strategic importance in the fight against the Sandinistas in Nicaragua, while the Sandinistas suffered a trade embargo throughout most of their time in government.

Armed uprisings, guerrilla warfare, strikes, and disruption are a constant threat to the developing economy and have jeopardized the potential of the Central American Common Market (CACM), created in 1960 by five of the republics. The most basic problem, however, is the limited number of products that the countries sell on the world market. Only Panama has a certain degree of security. This is because a high percentage of its foreign exchange comes from banking, offshore financial services, and revenue from both the Panama Canal and the new Trans-Isthmian pipeline that carries oil from the Pacific to the Atlantic.

Agriculture

Agriculture is the basis of the economy in all the Central American republics except Panama. Two of the principal crops, coffee and bananas, were

---

Drugs
The traffic in drugs is becoming an increasingly serious problem in Central America, particularly in Panama, which is on the direct route from the world's major suppliers in Colombia and South America to the markets of Miami and other parts of North America. In Belize law-enforcement agencies are unable to control the international cocaine traffickers who use the country as a trans-shipment route. As a problem cocaine now outranks marijuana, which has been grown in Belize for many years. Drug-related problems of corruption and violence are now evident in the major cities of both countries.

---

introduced in the last century and for many years remained the sole source of foreign exchange.

Coffee is grown in the highlands. Its successful cultivation has been particularly important in Costa Rica, Guatemala, and El Salvador, where it represents 60 percent of the value of the country's exports. The banana plantations are in the coastal lowlands and have been developed mostly by U.S. firms. The crop has grown to dominate the economy of the region to such a degree that the countries have become known as "banana republics." Bananas are still the number one export of Honduras and Panama. In Belize sugar has replaced timber as the country's main export.

All the countries have recognized the need to diversify their agricultural products, and tobacco, cotton, rice, cacao, spices, soybeans, peanuts, and vegetables are now also grown for export. In

For many years Central America produced mostly bananas and coffee. Recently there has been a move to diversify the economy, and in Costa Rica pineapples are now grown commercially.

most countries more than half the population is involved in agricultural work. The small farmers grow crops for their own use or for local markets and do not contribute significantly to the gross national product.

The profitable commercial farming is controlled by a few companies and wealthy landowners. In Guatemala 90 percent of the coffee is grown on just over a quarter of the plantations.

On the whole, attempts to redistribute land and make it profitable have not been successful. Only a percentage of the land is good for farming, but much of this is still not being cultivated, except in El Salvador, which intensively farms most of its arable land.

The fishing industry is small and lacks investment. Shrimp from the Pacific and Atlantic is the main catch, plus lobsters, shellfish, and conch. Panama now ranks as the world's third-largest shrimp exporter.

Mineral resources, industry, and power

Although all the Central American countries besides Belize have some mineral resources, few of these have been commercially exploited. The most common minerals are iron ore, copper, gold, and silver. Bauxite, the ore from which aluminum is extracted, is found in Nicaragua, Panama, and in Costa Rica, where the discovery of a valuable deposit prompted large-scale investment in an aluminum smelting plant. Honduras has probably the richest resources, with large deposits of tin, iron, copper, and coal. Panama has vast deposits of copper that are not being developed currently because of the world economic situation. The main mining activity in Panama is limited to the extraction of limestone, clays, sea salt, and semiprecious stones.

El Salvador and Guatemala are the two most industrially developed countries. Manufacturing is based on the agricultural economy, with firms involved in food processing and the production of textiles, shoes, leather goods, and tobacco. Other major industries include oil refining, cement, metals, electrical machinery, paper, and paper products. In Belize manufacturing is connected with the timber industry, producing furniture, telephone poles, resins, and veneers.

Oil also has to be imported, although some small deposits have been located and are being tapped. Hydroelectricity is being developed in various Central American countries, depending upon local economic and political circumstances. Currently, Honduras is able to export power to several of its neighbors, while El Salvador's plant on the Río Lempa, the first in Central America, has enabled the country to be self-sufficient in electricity.

Forestry and ranching

Throughout Central America there are vast areas of forest. In several countries forests cover about half the land. These are largely untapped for commercial purposes, despite the existence of

Almost everyone the world over has tried chewing gum. One of the basic ingredients comes from the sapodilla tree. In the forests of the Petén, Guatemala, the trees grow in isolated places and are tapped by chicleros, *who score the bark with machete cuts and then collect the sap, or chicle.*

91

Forests in Central America are being felled to create farmland. Not all forest is the species-rich rain forest, and some, like this dry tropical forest in Belize, is in far greater danger.

valuable hardwoods such as oak, mahogany, cedar, and rosewood. Chicle, used to make chewing gum, is obtained from the sapodilla tree, and Peruvian balsam, found only in El Salvador, is used for medicinal and industrial purposes.

The forests are, however, being exploited in a different way. Wood is used extensively as fuel in both Honduras and Nicaragua, and there are a number of sawmills for the production of plywood. The most serious and uncontrolled devastation of large areas of forests has taken place to allow for cattle grazing. In Panama large cattle farms have been established for a long time, and in the Guanacaste province of Costa Rica there are great cattle ranches.

Tourism

Tourism has great potential in Central America but is unlikely to develop until there is greater political stability in the region. The international tourist possibilities include archaeology, wildlife, diving and sailing off the Caribbean coast, beautiful scenic areas, fine colonial cities, the Indian peoples, and the Panama Canal.

In the ever-widening search to develop their economies, the countries of Central America have turned to tourism. Of prime importance to Guatemala and Belize is the Maya Trail, or La Ruta Maya, which will open archaeological sites and national wildlife parks to tourists.

In particular, Guatemala and Belize have a great deal to offer tourists. Within easy reach of Guatemala City are spectacular lakes and the bustling Indian markets. Off the Belize coast, the cays and coral reef are a tropical paradise of white sands and crystal-clear water superb for fishing, snorkeling, and diving. The largest of the cays, Ambergris, is only 35 miles (56 kilometers) north of Belize City.

Eco-tourism

The "green" 1990s have brought a new kind of tourist to the last wilderness areas of Central America. Eco-tourism is being developed to utilize the resources of the rain forests, beautiful coastlines, rivers, and volcanoes. Costa Rica has over 30 national parks and wildlife refuges. These places provide a rare opportunity to see an abundance of wildlife. In Guatemala the protected ecosystem of Mario Dary Rivera Park is less than three hours from the capital. Belize boasts a santuary for black howler monkeys, locally known as "baboons." The Baboon Sanctuary involves eight village communities, and each has agreed to give protection to the few remaining bands of monkeys that live on their land.

Conclusion

All of the countries of Central America are experiencing difficult times, and prospects for the future cannot be described as encouraging. Much will depend on the position adopted by the U.S. banks and by international agencies if Central America is to overcome its political and economic difficulties. During the last decade, and largely prompted by Nobel Prize-winner ex-President Arias of Costa Rica, some measures were proposed to bring peace to the region, and it must be hoped that future attempts will be made that are both workable and acceptable to all the republics. If peace and a stable government can be achieved, there is every possibility that the region's resources can be developed for the benefit of all the people of Central America.

Index

This edition originally published 1992 by
Heinemann Children's Reference, a division
of Heinemann Educational Books, Ltd.